1, 2, 3 ...

By the Sea

*In memory of my grandmother, Lillian Erickson Thornberg,
who gave me endless love, and to my cousin, Gloria Spencer
Beaver, who taught me how to look at clouds and life. – DM*

*To the windjammer "Isaac H. Evans" for some
great times by the sea. – HM*

Kane Miller, A Division of EDC Publishing
Text copyright © S. Dianne Moritz, 2013
Illustrations copyright © Hazel Mitchell, 2013

All rights reserved.
For information contact:
Kane Miller, A Division of EDC Publishing
PO Box 470663
Tulsa, OK 74147-0663
www.kanemiller.com
www.edcpub.com

Library of Congress Control Number: 2012935080

Manufactured by Regent Publishing Services, Hong Kong
Printed September 2012 in ShenZhen, Guangdong, China
1 2 3 4 5 6 7 8 9 10
ISBN: 978-1-935279-94-5

1, 2, 3 ...

By the Sea

A counting book

Written by Dianne Moritz
Illustrated by Hazel Mitchell

Kane Miller
A DIVISION OF EDC PUBLISHING

Mommy ...
me ...
and Max is three ...

… biking, hiking
by the sea.

Striped umbrellas in the sun ...
flapping, snapping.

We rent ONE.

1

Lots of towels: red, green, blue ...
lying, drying.

We have TWO.

Jellyfish float in the sea ...
swishy, squishy.

We find THREE.

Big waves tumble onto shore ...
crashing,

splashing.

We chase FOUR.

4

Seagulls fly and seagulls dive ...

squawking, flocking.

We spy FIVE.

Surfers surf and do surf tricks ...
lunging,

plunging.

We watch SIX.

6

Cotton clouds form up in heaven ...

drifting, shifting.

We see SEVEN.

7

Fishermen fish, using bait ...
reeling, creeling.

We count EIGHT.

We build towers in sunshine ...
sloppy,

gloppy.

We make NINE.

Plovers hide in beach-grass glen ...
peeping, sleeping.

We spot TEN.

10

HAMBURGERS! HOTDOGS!

ICE CREAM!
Race to snack-shack.

Stand in line.

Tummy yummy ...

Max wants mine!

Watch the sunset. Cool winds blow.
Cuddling, huddling ...

time to go!

Goodnight, sun.
Hello, new moon.
Later, 'gator.
Be back soon!